Bear Hug

For Fred Bear, with love xxx

First U.S. edition 2014

Library of Congress Catalog Card Number 2013955672
ISBN 978-0-7636-6630-9

TLF 19 18 17 16 15 14
10 9 8 7 6 5 4 3 2 1

Printed in Dongguan, Guangdong, China

This book was typeset in Palatino.
The illustrations were done in collage.

TEMPLAR BOOKS

an imprint of Candlewick Press
99 Dover Street
Somerville, Massachusetts 02144
www.candlewick.com

Bear Hug

Katharine McEwen

templar books

an imprint of Candlewick Press

Deep in the woods,
under snow-thick skies,
in a cave among the
whispering trees,
is a young bear.

Sniffing the wintry air,
he knows he must get ready
for the cold nights ahead.

So just as Papa showed him,
he gathers leaves and bundles of bracken
to make a warm winter bed.

And just as Mama showed him,
he dives into the shivery river
to catch fat, silvery fish.

Then, one day, he sees a friendly face
across the water—another young
bear like him.

Among the frosty moss and riverside rocks,
the two hungry bears share their catch.

As the days get colder, they gather berries
to fill their bellies, feasting
until they're full.

When the icy skies darken
and the snowflakes twirl and tumble,
the two bears lollopy-lumber back to the cave.

And there, against the shudder-cold night,
on a soft bracken bed, the bears stay snug
in a big bear hug.

All winter long, the bears sleep soundly.

The woods rest too,
under a deep, downy
blanket of snow.

Then, early one morning,
the bears are awoken by a bold
and beautiful sound.

They sniff the air.
It is warm and fresh, and the woodland
is brimming with birdsong.

Blinking in the sunshine,
they know that spring
has arrived at last.

And then from within the cave
comes another recent arrival,
as soft as thistledown
and lively as a sunbeam . . .

their little bear cub!

As the days grow longer and the nights get shorter, life fills the forest.

Bees buzz busily in honey-filled hives.

Fat, silvery fish swim in the river.

And then when the nights grow
longer and the days get shorter,

the cub gathers leaves,
just as Papa shows him.

And when the air gets colder
and frost nips at his nose,
the cub catches fish in the shivery river,
just as Mama shows him.

Day by day, he learns
everything he needs to be able
to venture out on his own.

But for now,
as the snows come
and the icy winds return,

it is time to settle down
for a long winter sleep.

Cozy in the cave,
safe until the spring,
they slumber—a little bear family,
warm and snug in a big bear hug.